All global publishing rights are held by

Ukiyoto Publishing

Published in 2024

Content Copyright © Ukiyoto

ISBN 9789361729126

All rights reserved.
No part of this publication may be reproduced, transmitted, or stored in a retrieval system, in any form by any means, electronic, mechanical, photocopying, recording or otherwise, without the prior permission of the publisher.

The moral rights of the author have been asserted.

This is a work of fiction. Names, characters, businesses, places, events, locales, and incidents are either the products of the author's imagination or used in a fictitious manner. Any resemblance to actual persons, living or dead, or actual events is purely coincidental.

This book is sold subject to the condition that it shall not by way of trade or otherwise, be lent, resold, hired out or otherwise circulated, without the publisher's prior consent, in any form of binding or cover other than that in which it is published.

www.ukiyoto.com

Contents

The Red Velvet Cake   1
By Juju's Pearls (Dr. Reemanshu Bansal)

An Eternity of Love   14
By Manmohan Sadana

Love Unfiltered   19
By Yogesh A Gupta

Sunflower Flowers   38
By Sabbani Laxminarayana

Faded Dandelions   42
By Riddhima Sen

Why   45
By Shaurya Prakash

First Love   49
By Purnima Dixit

About the Authors   *52*

The Red Velvet Cake
By Juju's Pearls (Dr. Reemanshu Bansal)

Prelude

All the famous love stories which we have read in our childhood and teenage years have never had a happy ending. One can pick any story be it of Heer-Ranjha, Laila-Manju, Shiri-Farhad, Sohni-Mahiwal, Romeo-Juliet, Bajirao-Mastani etc. All these love stories have a great beginning with painful separation and a cruel heart rendering end.

At times, I feel, why do we read such stories and what lessons do we learn. As a teenager, I had started believing that love was a disease, true love was rare and beyond reach of human beings. This had caused a negative association with emotional, love like feelings. However, life does change when one meets the soulmate. Lucky are the ones who find true love and get a chance to spend a life time. Let's see life through eyes of two teenagers Chaand and Bhanot.

Story

Every phase of life is beautiful. Birth, childhood, teenage and adulthood. A child wants to become a teenager, a teenager wants to become an adult. And, an adult wants to become a child. This is the circle of life.

The most tender age is of teenage. Hormonal spurts, physical changes, whirlpool of emotions and feeling of attraction towards the opposite gender. There are always few stories which are left unsaid, some stories move till high school. The luckiest ones are life long and they give a name to their relationship.

Chaand was a thirteen-year-old girl, studying in grade ninth in a public school in a metro city. Grade nine is a class, when many children change schools to pursue high school studies in a more competitive environment in the best schools. Chaand was a brilliant, all rounder type of girl, the most sort after student, both by teachers and her friends. Teachers entrusted her with many responsibilities in addition to academics.

Spring time is the best time of the year with flowers blooming everywhere. Promotion to new class in High school building. There were always few admissions in the second week of the new academic session, A routine Monday morning was about to herald a beautiful spring in Chaand's heart, touch her soul. She was totally unaware of it.

School bell rang, everyone came into the playground for morning prayers. As Chaand was rushing past the students to go to the podium for the morning news, she felt a tap on her shoulder. She shrugged and looked back impatiently. Her feet froze and heart skipped a beat as she saw an extremely handsome boy with subtle moustache and warm smile. He said, "Sorry! For tapping, please tie your shoelaces else you will fall and never make it to the podium", he smiled and winked as he said, "New admission, grade IX-A."

Morning assembly went well. Chaand had almost forgotten the incident. When she reached her class, she saw the same boy sitting on the same desk as hers. She smiled and said, "Hey, I am Chaand, thank you for today morning." He smiled and replied, "Hello, I am Bhanot, new admission. Principal Sir told me to sit with Chaand. And now I feel I am very lucky."

When the Class teacher came, new admissions introduced themselves. Teacher told Chaand to help Bhanot and two other students. For the first time, Chaand experienced butterflies in her stomach and a vague sense of dizziness. She thought the feeling might be related to her menstrual cycle timing. The first week went off well.

As if God had some plans, Bhanot's residence was in the same area as Chaand. So, they started going by the same school bus. The time they were spending together was gradually increasing, In the evenings, they started going to each other's house for exchange of notes, books, novels etc. When school closed for summer vacation, they both joined the Club in their locality for swimming and badminton classes.

They had got used to each other's company so much that other students started making stories about them. They were oblivious as they thought they were just friends. Their friend circle became smaller as they felt complete whenever they were together. In school, too, teachers unknowingly made them partners in school house projects, elocution and other extra-curricular activities. Their pair became the winning pair in inter school competitions. The year flew at the snap of the finger.

On the day of the final term result, Bhanot told Chaand about his father's transfer and him going to another city, another school. He had lived life hopping from city to city, changing schools as his father was in the Army. Chaand became emotional and could not control back her tears. She started avoiding him for the next few days. There was a delay in transfer orders, so Bhanot continued in the same school in grade tenth.

Bhanot could not understand Chaand's behaviour and he felt hurt. Gradually, they started sitting on separate desks, ate lunch alone and seldom sat in the same seat in the school bus. His fathers transfer orders came and he knew he had another term before he would be shifted to another school.

One day Bhanot asked Chaand out for a walk and coffee. Chaand refused. On Bhanot's constant request, she agreed. Over coffee, they spoke causally drifting from topics and never seeing each other in the eyes. Finally, Bhanot spoke up, "Hey Chaand, why are you acting so arrogant. I am the one who should be upset with you. After all, you never replied to my letter. And I still don't know how you feel about me!". Chaand was shocked and she spoke in a fumbled voice, "What are you saying? Which letter are you talking about!" she gave a questioning look.

"Oh! So now I can clearly visualize the entire situation. Don't try to be naïve. I had placed a letter in your birthday card and had given to your house helper to place it on your study table. You never mentioned nor replied. Even after I told you my father has been transferred, you never ever discussed or mentioned about my letter. Do you know, I insisted on staying back on the pretext of continuing the term as I wanted to know why you did this to me," spoke Bhanot looking sad and shaken.

Suddenly, Chaand got up from her chair and told Bhanot to wait for her. She rushed towards her home, she went straight to her room and started searching her study table and room. She checked her birthday cards but could not find any letter. She believed Bhanot and always knew something was there between the two of them. Their chemistry was very strong and they bonded like soul mates. She turned on her mobile flashlight and started searching for the letter. Finally, she saw a white tip underneath her bed. She had a box bed and there was hardly an inch space between the floor and the box bed. Anything could easily slide beneath the bed and remain hidden till the time the bed was pushed for the annual cleaning process. She pushed her bed and finally saw a letter. The outer cover was inked in red as BC. With trembling hands, she opened it. Tears started flowing down her cheeks as she read it.

The Letter

Dear Chaand,

I am really grateful to you for all your help which helped a newcomer like me adjust in a new school in a new environment. I enjoy every moment whenever we are together. Now my father's transfer orders have come. Earlier, I used to look forward for new postings, new places. Now I am feeling sad. I am unable to understand the emotional turmoil I am going through. I know you consider me as a friend and nothing beyond, I want to confess that I have developed feelings for you more than that of a friend.

I am unsure about the whole thing. This has happened for the very first time that I think about morning time, when I will be with you. Is this love or just a teenage infatuation? Whatever it may be, I feel happy and complete when I am with you.

It has required lot of courage to write this letter and ask you -Do you feel more than a friend or just a friend. Whatever is your answer please reply by ordering a red velvet cake at your birthday party.

Waiting for your answer,

Yours, Bhanot.

Chaand read this letter number of times and finally remembered Bhanot must be waiting at the café. She rode her bicycle with a great speed and reached the Cafe.

Panting she said, "Sorry! I never got your letter on my birthday. It had slid down my bed and that space is not routinely cleaned. Now that I have read it, All I want to say is -Let's order a red velvet cake," And she gave a big smile. Bhanot blushed and Chaand found it amusing. Bhanot seemed tongue tied and didn't utter a word.

For the first time, they saw in each other's eyes and smiled. They knew they were too young for the emotions and feelings they were experiencing for each other. In their heart they knew they were smitten by teenage love and the space seemed wonderful and too good to be true.

From next day onwards, their behaviour became normal. They shared the same desk, lunch, same seat in school bus etc. They made a promise to work hard and score good marks. Bhanot extended his stay and urged his parents to let him complete his grade tenth. His parents found it reasonable. His father left while his mother stayed back for his board exams.

After board exams, Chaand had to leave to a bigger city for her competitive entrance studies. Bhanot had to join an International Board school as per his parent's choice. They wanted him to do Majors in physics from a renowned US university. When the time came to go in their respective directions, Chaand and Bhanot met and decided upon few things in their relationship. This distance would be the greatest test. They decided to meet after grade twelfth, after securing admission in the colleges of their own choice. The two-year separation was the real test of their love. They had promised to keep no contact with each other.

Two years flew by and time came for their reunion meeting. Bhanot had faired well and had successfully convinced his parents to do under graduation from home country. He had promised to go to USA for masters. He had admission letter from one of the top universities of his home country in the same city where Chaand was likely to go for her graduation

On the other side, Chaand had shown the brighter side of studying graduation in USA to her parents. After many rounds of talks and discussion, her parents were finally convinced. She had taken the required exams and had acceptance letter from a very good university in US in the same city where Major in Physics university was. It seemed like a fool proof plan.

As they both headed to Chaand's hometown, they felt very happy with their college admissions. Bhanot was feeling happy to be in motherland and be close to his love. On the other hand, Chaand was super excited to take the flight of her dreams into the arms of her lover.

They reached the Café almost at the same time and spoke in unison, "Please give a red velvet cake. They looked at each other with love. Hormonal changes in later teens had turned Chaand into a beautiful young girl and Bhanot looked like a handsome young man with little moustache and beard near temples.

They ordered their favourite coffee - French Vanilla latte and exchanged the cakes. Finally, Bhanot spoke, "So Chaand speak up about your two-year journey. I am eagerly impatiently waiting to hear you and tell my side too." Chaand's eyes lit up as she said, "You won't believe, I convinced my parents about pursuing studies in US. Look, I have acceptance letters from a couple of universities. We will in the same country and most likely same city. We will try to meet as often as possible."

Hearing this, Bhanot's jaw dropped open and cake fell out of his mouth. "You don't seem to be happy!" Chaand asked softly. Bhanot kept the cake aside and pulled out his college admission letter. He told her about convincing his parents to do his graduation from home country so that he would be able to spend time with her.

There was stony silence. Their situation was same as earlier, only the person had been switched. Chaand dug her spoon into the pastry cake and signalled him to open his mouth. "Let's celebrate our admissions", and she offered him a piece of their favourite red velvet cake.

They went for a movie, spent a great evening trying to behave as if everything was alright. The happy part was that the separation of two years had deepened their love for each other. And their admission letters were a living proof. Deep inside they knew their teenage love had matured and it was indeed love and not mere infatuation.

They thought about talking to their parents regarding this situation. Later shelved it as at the age of eighteen, parents will lecture them on focussing their career and not get involved in a relationship. Soon, the time came for Chaand to go abroad. Meanwhile Bhanot had done lot of research and spoken to his teachers regarding migration to US university during second year of his course.

It was again a question of staying away for another year. This time they kept a constant communication. At the end of first year, Bhanot got a scholarship under international student exchange program. He wanted to surprise Bhanot. Happy to meet his lady love after yet another one year, he took a direct non-stop flight.

With the aim of surprising his love, he reached her place of stay. The lights were off and it was all calm and dark. Fearing the worst, he slowly pushed the main door. There was a loud bang, he felt a shower of flowers on his head. The overhead light lit up the centre table with focus on the box on the table. As he opened the box, he saw a heart shaped red velvet cake with two initials on top "CB, Welcome to US."

He felt a hug from behind. He pulled her by the arms and saw a smiling Chaand. She laughed aloud and said, "Surprise! look the person planning to surprise his love was surprised by his own love."

Bhanot gave a questioning look," How did you know about my plans" This was kept as a secret." She gave him a cuddly hug and said, "Technology my dear, you had switched your location on when you had booked a cab for airport. You forgot to switch it off. All this while, I knew your path."

He continued, "And the path leads into the arms of my love."

They both sat on the couch and enjoyed their favourite cake with their French Vanilla coffee.

Their teenage love story had stood the test of time and matured into a bond of a life time.

An Eternity of Love

By Manmohan Sadana

On Valentine's Day in 2024, a couple in their sixties sat on a balcony in Oberoi Apartments on Mall Road, sipping tea from Japanese porcelain cups. Between them lay a handmade rose, evoking memories of a bygone era. With each sip of Lipton tea, their minds flashed back four decades...

In bustling Delhi, on a distinctive Valentine's Day in 1984, the air was charged with love and anticipation. Amid the vibrant chaos, a unique love story unfolded between Arjun, a boy with dyslexia but a fervor for art and literature, and Aisha, a blind girl with a heart brimming with dreams.

Arjun, a former student of the "School of Aspiration: Dada-Dadi Foundation" in South Delhi, had enrolled in St. Stephen's College at the University of Delhi. Simultaneously, Aisha, a student at Hope Blind School in Gurgaon, also joined the same course and college. Destiny brought them to share a table in class, situated at the corner next to the door. In their first class, Professor Almedia Pattison asked students to introduce themselves, during which Arjun continuously murmured "Aisha!" in a mellowed tone, unnoticed by the professor but perplexing Aisha.

Their initial conversations revolved around the plays and novels in their literature course, discussing the intricacies of works such as Sophocles' "Antigone" and Homer's "Odyssey." Despite being verbally expressive, they faced challenges in writing due to their special abilities, relying on scribes for tutorials and exams, where they consistently scored well.

As weeks turned into months, Arjun and Aisha's connection deepened. Their first year in college felt like an eternity of togetherness, with IQ and EQ levels surpassing those of their peers. The Delhi winter and the new year heralded the onset of romance, marked by subtle touches and shared moments over tea near Ramjas College or bhelpuri outside Delhi School of Economics.

The winter unfolded their relationship into a more romantic realm. The touch of fingers, holding hands while crossing roads, created a tingling sensation within them. A symphony of butterflies fluttered as their young hearts navigated the uncharted waters of affection and attraction, marking the transformative journey into innocence and passion.

One day, Arjun proposed an outing to watch the movie "Love at First Sight," based on the book "The Statistical Probability of Love at First Sight." Aisha agreed, and the two anticipated spending quality time together in the corner seat of a Delhi movie hall. The two hours spent watching the movie left an indelible mark on their lives, with the only remembrance being Aisha laying her head on Arjun's shoulder with her eyes shut.

As January raced by, the couple eagerly awaited Valentine's Day. Arjun nervously crafted a beautiful rose from clay, intending to express his feelings to Aisha. The day began with Arjun presenting the carefully crafted rose to Aisha, who felt the beauty through her heightened senses. Their day unfolded across various locations in Delhi, discovering a unique connection beyond conventional understanding.

In a park near the University of Delhi, Arjun described vibrant colors, warm sunlight, and rustling leaves, while Aisha shared the symphony of sounds around them. The exchange transcended physical limitations, fostering a profound connection. As the sun set, Arjun took Aisha to a rooftop, describing the night sky and stars, creating vivid imagery that Aisha felt within.

In the quiet moments between dialogues, Arjun and Aisha embraced a profound connection that transcended spoken language. Under the starlit sky on the roof of 'One 8 Commune' restaurant at Mall Road, Arjun whispered his proposal, and Aisha, with a warm smile, accepted. Their love story unfolded—a testament to the power of connection between two specially gifted individuals, understanding each other and finding beauty when two hearts beat in unison. Time seemed to pause as they shared a delicate moment under the starlit sky, promising a lifetime of new adventures.

A renowned mystic poet has said,

"Escaping from the eyes of the stars

and the glances of the flowers,

Two hearts met in the waning

of the night."

***

Love Unfiltered
Finding Trust and Devotion in Today's Swipe-Right World

By Yogesh A Gupta

The love stories of Radha, Meera Bai, and Draupadi with Lord Krishna are timeless tales that define a profound and spiritual form of love, transcending ordinary boundaries. These narratives, often seen as super teenage love stories, showcase the depth and intensity of devotion and connection between these extraordinary women and the divine Krishna.

Radha, often considered the eternal beloved of Krishna, embodies selfless and unconditional love. Her love is passionate, yet spiritual, symbolizing the union of the soul with the divine. Radha's dedication to Krishna becomes a source of inspiration, depicting an ethereal and boundless connection that goes beyond the ordinary realms of human love.

Meera Bai, the saintly poet-princess, expressed her love for Krishna through her poignant poems and devotional songs. Her unwavering devotion and the symbolic marriage to the divine showcase a unique and transformative form of love. Meera's story is a testament to the idea that true love transcends societal norms and is an inner journey of the soul towards the divine.

Draupadi, a revered queen in the Mahabharata, shares a special bond with Krishna. Amidst the complexities of her life, Draupadi's love for Krishna is a steadfast anchor. The episode of Krishna saving Draupadi during her cheer-haran exemplifies the protective and caring aspect of their relationship. It is a tale of trust, friendship, and unwavering support.

On the other side, Lord Krishna's love for Radha, Meera Bai, and Draupadi is portrayed as a divine and all-encompassing force. It reflects the concept of God as the ultimate lover, responding to the sincere devotion and love of his devotees. Krishna's interactions with Radha, his divine play with Meera Bai, and his role as a confidant and protector of Draupadi exemplify the multifaceted nature of his love.

These stories, although rooted in ancient scriptures, carry universal themes that resonate across generations, including the teenage audience. The tales of Radha, Meera Bai, and Draupadi with Krishna showcase love as a spiritual journey, emphasizing qualities such as devotion, selflessness, and the divine connection that goes beyond the boundaries of age and time. They inspire a profound understanding of love that is transformative, pure, and eternal.

Can anyone love better than Radha

In the enchanting realm of Vrindavan in village of Barsana, where the air resonates with tales of love and devotion, the divine narrative of Radha unfolded. Born into the embrace of the loving couple, Vrishbhanhu and Ratnagarbha Devi, Radha's entry into the world was marked by a peculiar destiny – closed eyes that veiled her sight in a shroud of mystery.

Undaunted by the challenge, Radha's parents embarked on a pilgrimage of prayers and austerities, their hearts yearning for a miraculous intervention. The passing of five arduous years cast a shadow of despair, until a fortuitous invitation extended to Nanda Baba and Yashoda, accompanied by their son Krishna, altered the course of Radha's fate.

As the visitors entered the sacred abode, Radha sensed an otherworldly presence guiding her closed eyes.

Radha: (with closed eyes, expressing wonder) "Mother, I sense something extraordinary, an unseen force pulling me towards it".

Ratnagarbha Devi: (smiling) "Perhaps it's a divine blessing, my child. Let it guide you".

Nanda Baba: (warmly) "Vrishbhanhu, we bring greetings and the joy of our little Krishna".

Vrishbhanhu: "Welcome, dear friends. Radha, come, greet our guests".

Radha: (guided by an unseen force, moving towards Krishna) "Krishna, I feel your presence".

Krishna: (smiling) "Radha, in your darkness, let my light be your sight".

Radha: (opening her eyes for the first time) "The world is more beautiful than I ever imagined, and your smile, Krishna, is the source of this newfound vision".

Krishna: "Radha, in every lifetime, in every story, you and I are bound together. Our love will endure through time, an eternal symphony in the heart of Vrindavan".

As days passed the bond became strong.

Krishna: (with determination)" Mother, I wish to marry Radha. Send a marriage proposal to her house".

Yashoda: (laughs) "Krishna, is this another one of your playful pranks?"

Krishna: (insistent) "No, Mother, it's my sincere desire. I cannot imagine anyone else as my companion".

Yashoda: (serious) "Krishna, it's not that simple. Radha is engaged to Aiyyan, and there are other reasons. She's older, of lower status, and some even say she's too bold for our family".

Krishna: (warningly) "Mother, if you deny my request, you risk losing your son".

Nand: (calmly) "Krishna, consider one of the chieftain's daughters. They would make suitable wives".

Krishna: (adamant) "No, Father. It's Radha alone who holds my heart".

Nand: (postponing the decision) "Sage Garg is to arrive tomorrow. We'll seek his guidance in this matter".

Sage Garg: (wise) "Krishna, marriage involves considerations like family backgrounds, temperaments, and future plans".

Krishna: (defiant) "Radha fulfills all these criteria for me, revered sage".

Sage Garg: (decisive) "It's time you learn the purpose of your birth. You are the eighth son of Devki and Vasudev, destined to free the Yadava race from Kansa's tyranny".

Krishna: (shocked) "What about my desire to marry Radha?"

Sage Garg: (enlightening) "Your task demands a grander commitment. Forget about a normal life in Vrindavan; your destiny is to be a savior of the entire human race".

As the truth of Krishna's divine purpose unfolded, the weight of his destiny bore down upon him. Radha's dreams of a life together shattered, and the echoes of separation reverberated through the sacred land of Vrindavan. The divine love and sacrifice had just begun, leaving Krishna torn between his heart's desire and the cosmic duty he was born to fulfill.

Krishna: (with a somber tone) :Radha, the time has come for us to part ways, and I wish to leave you with a lasting memory".

Radha: (with love in her eyes) "Krishna, you need not give me anything. Our love is already etched in my heart".

Krishna: (smiling) "I want to dedicate something special to you, something that encapsulates the essence of our love".

As Krishna unveils his bansuri (flute), a hush falls over the divine surroundings.

Krishna: (softly) "This melody, Radha, is just for you. It's the final chapter of our love story".

The bansuri starts playing, its notes weaving a tapestry of emotions.

Radha: (overwhelmed) "Krishna, your music is divine, just like our love. But why dedicate your final play to me?"

Krishna: (with deep affection) "Radha, this bansuri holds the echoes of our shared moments, the laughter, the tears, and the unspoken words. I promise you, after today, it shall remain silent. Our love deserves a melody that resonates in eternity".

Radha, touched by Krishna's gesture, listens to the hauntingly beautiful tune, her heart intertwined with the music.

Radha: (teary-eyed) "Krishna, our love is beyond the ordinary. It is a devotion that transcends time and form. Your last play is etched in my soul, a treasure I shall carry even in our separation".

Krishna: (whispering) "Radha, our souls are bound by a love that surpasses the physical realm. Even in our parting, our connection shall endure".

As the final notes of the bansuri fade away, Krishna gazes into Radha's eyes, their love immortalized in the lingering echoes of the divine melody.

This scene encapsulates the essence of Radha and Krishna's love—a sacred bond that goes beyond the worldly and ordinary, a connection of devotion and purity that remains unbroken even in the face of separation. The bansuri becomes a symbol of their eternal love, its last notes echoing in the hearts of those who witness the divine union of Radha and Krishna.

In the sacred city of Dwarka, after years of an unwavering connection that transcended time and space, Radha, now aged and fragile, felt an irresistible pull to see Krishna one last time. Free from the shackles of domestic responsibilities, she embarked on a poignant journey, traversing the distance to Krishna's palace.

Arriving at the divine abode, Radha, though weak in body, bore an ethereal beauty that mirrored the purity of her love. As she caught a glimpse of Devakinandan, Lord Krishna, her heart swelled with awe at the godly radiance that surrounded him.

In the twilight of her existence, Krishna, recognizing the depth of Radha's devotion, approached her with a tender query.

Krishna: "Radha, what is your heart's desire? You may make a wish".

Radha: (with grace) "Krishna, I ask for no worldly desires. Instead, I seek the eternal melody of your divine flute, to accompany my soul through days and nights".

In that sacred moment, Radha surrendered herself to the enchanting tunes that resonated from Krishna's bansuri. The music echoed not just through the palace but reached the depths of Radha's soul, intertwining with the devotion that had defined her existence.

As the last notes lingered in the air, Radha, in a sublime act of surrender, transcended the mortal realm. Her physical form dissolved, and her soul merged spiritually with Krishna, the culmination of a love story that had weathered the trials of separation.

Witnessing Radha's departure, Krishna, unable to bear the weight of the heartbreak, took his cherished flute and broke it symbolically. The divine music, once an expression of their love, now silenced in the wake of Radha's departure.

This love story, born in the innocence of childhood and matured through the trials of separation, stands as an eternal testament to the essence of love – a journey of selfless surrender and devotion. Radha, who now echoes through the ages as Radhe, signifies the embodiment of unconditional love, a beacon for generations to understand that true love lies in surrendering, not in capturing. The essence of

Krishna is incomplete without the presence of Radha, forever entwined in the tapestry of eternal love.

Can anyone devote herself like Mirabai?

Once upon a time in a faraway kingdom called Jodhpur, there lived a little princess named Mirabai. She was the granddaughter of a kind man named Rao Dudaji, who was part of the Rathod Dynasty.

When Mirabai was just four years old, she saw a big wedding parade and asked her mom, "Mom, who will be my husband someday?" Her mom pointed at a picture of Lord Krishna and said, "My dear Meera, Lord Krishna will be your husband." From then on, Mirabai loved and admired Lord Krishna a lot.

Sadly, when Mirabai was about 7 years old, her mom passed away. Later, her dad, Ratnasingh, fought in a battle to protect the kingdom from a ruler named Akbar, but he didn't come back.

Even though Mirabai didn't get much love from her parents, her grandpa, Rao Dudaji, took good care of her. He became like a second dad, showing her lots of love and support.

And so, with her love for Lord Krishna and the care of her wonderful grandfather, Mirabai's journey as a princess began.

In the royal court one day, a wise sadhu came to visit Mirabai's family. Mira was fascinated when she saw a beautiful little idol of Sri Krishna that the saint carried with him. The sadhu held it close to his heart, worshipped it with devotion, chanted mantras, sang songs, and even danced joyfully in front of it.

Rao Dudaji (RD): "Ah, esteemed Sadhu, your presence graces our court today. What brings you to our humble abode?"

Sadhu (S): "Greetings, noble Rao Dudaji. I have traveled far and wide, and my journey led me to share some wisdom with your esteemed family".

Mira (M): (Excitedly) "Grandpa, look! The sadhu has a beautiful idol of Lord Krishna!"

RD: "Indeed, it is a divine presence. Sadhu, tell us about this sacred idol you carry".

S: "This, dear Rao Dudaji, is a blessed Murti of Sri Krishna. It brings me immense joy and solace in my prayers and devotions".

M: (Eagerly) "Grandpa, I want one too! Can I have this idol, please?"

RD: (Smiling) "Mira, we must respect the sadhu's belongings. He carries this idol for his worship".

M: (Pouting) "But Grandpa, I want to worship Lord Krishna just like him!"

S: (Kindly)" Young one, the love in your heart is admirable. Perhaps, with your grandfather's permission, you can have a Murti of your own".

RD: (Thoughtfully) Sadhu, I promise to arrange for another idol for you. Would you consider parting with this one for the joy of my granddaughter?"

S: (Reluctantly) "Rao Dudaji, for the love of the divine, I shall share this Murti with your dear Mira".

RD: (Gratefully) "Thank you, noble Sadhu. Mira, this idol is now yours. Learn from the sadhu how to worship and cherish it".

M: (Excitedly) "Thank you, Grandpa! I'll take good care of it, just like the sadhu".

This marked the beginning of Mirabai's devotion, Mira, overjoyed, paid meticulous attention to the details of the worship, embracing the newfound joy of having her own idol of Shree Krishna.

When Mirabai turned sixteen, something happened that she didn't get to choose. In those times, people often united kingdoms through marriages. Rana Sangram Singh, the ruler of Mewar, had four sons, and he suggested that his son, Kumar Bhojraj, marry Mira. This proposal aimed to bring together two powerful Rajput kingdoms. Sadly, girls like Mira didn't have much say in their marriages back then. After the wedding, she refused to let Prince Bhojraj come close to her because she believed she was already married. Her heart belonged to Sri Krishna.

At first, Mira's family didn't take her unusual behavior seriously. They hoped she would change her mind, knowing that displeasing the powerful Sisodias wasn't a good idea. They tried to persuade her, made threats, attempted to make her suffer, and even considered harming her. But Mira stayed firm in her devotion to Sri Krishna. Mirabai was young, started a special journey inside herself, exploring spiritual things that would make her famous in India. She and her husband Bhojraj had a good friendship. Bhojraj liked her poems about Sri Krishna so much that he even agreed to build a temple for Sri Krishna in their palace.

Sadly, Bhojraj passed away in a battle in 1526. This really affected Mirabai because she lost her friend and someone who understood and protected her. Bhojraj didn't have any children.

People who didn't understand Mirabai tried to harm her. They sent her a basket with a poisonous snake –, it turned out to be an idol of Sri Krishna with flowers. Another time, they gave her bowl full of poison, but when Mirabai shared it with Sri Krishna, it turned into nectar. There was even a bed of nails sent to her, but when Mirabai lay on it, it turned into a bed of roses!

Young Mira faced many challenges, including attempts to harm her, but she remained devoted to her beloved Krishna. When things became too difficult, she decided to leave for Vrindavan, the place where Krishna had played with the Gopis and Radhika. In Vrindavan, Mira sought guidance from a knowledgeable sadhu, but he refused to see her because of a vow against meeting women. However, Mira reminded him that in Vrindavan, everyone is a Gopi, whether male or female, playing with the Creator, Shree Krishna. The sadhu realized his mistake, came out, and bowed down to Mira.

Throughout her life, Mira's style of expressing her love for Krishna was filled with passion, defiance, longing, anticipation, joy, and the ecstasy of union, always centered around her beloved Krishna.

The love story of Mira and Krishna imparts timeless lessons for today's teenagers. It encourages authenticity and self-expression, urging them to stay true to their beliefs and passions in the face of societal expectations. Mira's courageous journey emphasizes the importance of following one's heart and making choices aligned with personal convictions. The story underscores the power of unwavering devotion, resilience in overcoming challenges, and the recognition of inner divinity. It challenges gender norms, promoting equality and respect. Ultimately, Mira and Krishna's tale inspires teenagers to embrace their true selves, navigate life with courage and determination, nurture their spiritual well-being, and appreciate the richness of cultural diversity.

A man and a woman can be just friends. Learn from Draupadi and Krishna

Once upon a time in the legendary land of Panchaal, King Drupada faced a sorrowful defeat that would shape the destiny of his kingdom. It all began when Arjuna, the skilled warrior and disciple of Dronacharya, fought on behalf of his guru and triumphed over King Drupada, leading to the unfortunate loss of half the kingdom. The humiliated king harbored a burning desire for revenge against Dronacharya.

Determined to turn the tides of fortune, King Drupada embarked on a path of vengeance. He decided to perform a grand yajna, a sacred ritual seeking divine intervention to further his lineage and give rise to a formidable force that could bring down Dronacharya. With a heart filled with determination and the flames of the yajna soaring high, King Drupada's prayers were answered.

From the consecrated fire emerged his son, Dhrishtadyumna, a powerful and valiant warrior destined to avenge the kingdom's loss. However, the divine intervention didn't end there. Alongside Dhrishtadyumna, appeared a radiant and extraordinary princess, who would later be known as Draupadi or Panchali. Draupadi, the ethereal princess, grew up to be a symbol of beauty, intelligence, and resilience.

In the sacred city of Dwarka, where the waves of devotion resonated through the air and the magnificence of Lord Krishna's divine abode graced the shores, a touching incident unfolded between the revered Draupadi and the Lord himself. It is said that during one of Draupadi's visits to Dwarka, the resplendent residence of Lord Krishna, an incident occurred that would forever bind their hearts in a beautiful bond of friendship. The divine atmosphere of Dwarka was filled with the celestial aura of the Supreme Being, and Draupadi, overwhelmed by the divine presence, found herself in an unforgettable moment with the Lord.

In an intimate setting, Lord Krishna was delicately cutting fruits, his nimble fingers gracefully maneuvering the blade. However, in a rare instance, a slip occurred, and the sharp edge caused Krishna's finger to start bleeding. The sight of the blood invoked an immediate and instinctive reaction from Draupadi, who, in a moment of pure devotion and concern, rushed to Krishna's side. With a heart full of love and a swift movement, Draupadi tore a piece of cloth from the edge of her saree and tenderly wrapped it around Krishna's wounded finger, staunching the flow of blood. Her actions reflected not just her devotion but also her compassionate and caring nature. Krishna, charmed and touched by Draupadi's endearing gesture, gazed at her with the warmth that only a true friend could feel. Grateful for her selfless act, Lord Krishna, in his divine magnanimity, asked Draupadi what she desired in return for her kind deed. To this, Draupadi, the faithful devotee with unwavering love for her friend, responded with a request as profound as it was simple. She expressed her heart's desire that Krishna be a part of her life forever.

In that sacred moment, amidst the echoes of their divine friendship, Krishna and Draupadi forged a bond that transcended the realms of ordinary connections. Their friendship became a testament to the deep, unspoken understanding between a devotee and the Divine, a bond that withstood the tests of time and circumstance. And so, in Dwarka, the city of divine love, the enchanting tale of Krishna and Draupadi's everlasting friendship unfolded, leaving an indelible mark in the tapestry of timeless devotion. And this act itched in Indian memory till date when we celebrate festival of rakshabandhan.

In the present time, love stories like Radha, Meera, and Draupadi with Krishna, characterized by deep spiritual and emotional connections, may not be as common in the mainstream. However, there are still instances of enduring and meaningful relationships where individuals prioritize trust, loyalty, and devotion. While modern relationships often face different challenges and dynamics, the essence of authentic and profound love remains relevant. Some people seek lasting connections that go beyond superficial aspects, emphasizing mutual respect, understanding, and support, even in the age of social media and changing relationship norms.

Sunflower Flowers

By Sabbani Laxminarayana

"I loved that girl with all my heart, and she also loved me. There wasn't a single day that she could not live without seeing me," said my friend Sudhakar.

"Really!" I exclaimed.

"The other day she fell on me and wept bitterly," he shared again.

"Why?" I inquired.

"She can't live without me; she doesn't need anything without me. She can't marry anyone else but me only," he expressed with great affection towards her. This is the love story of our Sudhakar.

Our Sudhakar, in his early twenties, is pursuing his degree, while the girl is sixteen to seventeen. Falling in love is natural at that age, and due to the proximity of their two houses, their attention fell on each other. This boy saw that girl, and that girl saw this boy, and that's how their love story began.

However, I once advised Sudhakar, "Love is a mutual attraction, natural at this age. It is only your illusion that the girl will not live a single day without seeing you. If their elder brother, father, or relative notices this thing and scolds the girl and confronts you, then the girl will not come to show her face to you. If it comes to a situation where everyone knows about this love affair, the girl will always look out for her safety. A girl in a family living with dignity will not let others know about this love story. Society is not yet mature enough to understand your love. So, don't think of love and marriage; put a full stop to this love story and forget that girl, stay away from her," I advised.

Sudhakar did not understand my advice. He insisted, "That girl is not like that; she will give her life for me."

"What else did you see in her that made you love her?" I asked.

"Seeing that girl's heart, and seeing that girl's beauty," he fondly replied. When asked about their future plans, he said, "We want to get married in the future."

Three months passed. During this time, they spent time together, visiting temples, walking in parks, dining in hotels, and watching movies. However, one day, Sudhakar and the girl were discovered in a park by the girl's relatives. They beat Sudhakar, took the girl, and left.

Sudhakar returned home from the hospital with white bandages. Lying on the bed, he shed tears remembering the girl, hoping she would come for him. Despite waiting, the girl did not appear. Disappointed, Sudhakar sought her, but his hopes were in vain. The girl was nowhere to be found, and Sudhakar became despondent.

On an auspicious day, the girl got married and moved on with her life. Months and years passed as a routine. Sudhakar shared that whenever she appeared, she would walk away like a stranger without noticing him. Over time, Sudhakar also changed, got married, and settled in life. They both seemed to me like sunflowers following the sun as time passed.

Faded Dandelions

By Riddhima Sen

Faded Dandelions
My love, do you still remember
The days of explicit bliss;
When we were companions,
Bosom companions who could never be separated.
Lovers for an eternal timespan,

I still remember,
The warm smell of your blue cotton t-shirt,
The comfortable space in the lawn
Where we used to talk our hearts out,
Now, you have abandoned me
We may never be united again,
But, the memory of the sultry evening
Clinging to the fabric of your nylon cardigan
My pink sweater,
Continues to be persistent

Down my memory lane
The elegant view of the cherry blossoms
Strewn in my heart,
Light pinkish speckles
On my bleeding heart,
People go away,
But memories remain.

Although my heartstrings are baked with blood,
And embellished with the innards of my faint heart
I still cherish the memories of La Amour.
The dandelions have faded, beloved
White and shrunken.

Why

By Shaurya Prakash

What is this irony that
you've trapped me, Darling.
you convinced me to stay
but you went far away.
the air is getting cold and
everything seems smeared with forgotten love
without the brightness of your smile
the red is fading into pink while I sit here
drinking your favourite drink.

The flowers look withered, and the trees look dry.
I'll say this, Darla, I never thought you'd be one to make me cry.
It's Christmas Eve, it's chilled, but I lie here without a blanket
or a shoulder to weep on
without you now that you're gone
My heart feels shrivelled; my eyes feel sore

Every shade of blue I try to remember,
every speck of silver I see,
If I smell your perfume even
in the slightest at all...
Every bit of it makes me miss you so much more
and my heart keeps asking me
"Where did she go, the one you called doll?"

They're growing cold; my heart and soul.
Why did you go away Darla when you promised
to love me till I became frail, and you got old?
The bottle of Perrier is half-filled, just
like the rest of my life.
Where did you go my lovely,
what hid behind your cheeky smile,
your pretty face and your wistful eyes?
Why did you go away, Darla?
Was it something I did?
something I said.
I remember saying "I'll love you till death",
is that why my love, you left me here for dead?

The bedsheet is still crinkled.
On your side of the bed, remember that photo we took.
It's still up on that wall.
Where did you go away Darla,
my life, my love, my doll.

First Love

By Purnima Dixit

Sushant added another card to the treasure box, a tradition he had embraced since moving to the city and joining the art school last year. Without fail, every 14th of the month, he would receive these cards and gifts. Initially surprised, he soon found himself looking forward to these regular tokens of affection, especially the ones adorned with beautiful handwritten quotes.

He couldn't deny that he loved these cards, especially since the quotes seemed to align with his mood. Whether he felt low or needed motivation, the quotes never failed to cheer him up. Sometimes, they praised his smiles, his eyes, or simply wished him a good day.

Despite his curiosity, Sushant tried hard to discover the identity of his secret admirer. He wondered if it was one of his students from the art school, someone from the neighborhood, an acquaintance, or even a stranger. The mysterious cards somehow always reached him, be it outside his door, in his bag, or on his table in the staff room.

On the 14th of this month, he decided to take an off from the art school to unravel the mystery. As the late evening approached, he had yet to receive the day's gift. Somewhere in his heart, disappointment lingered, not just because the gift hadn't arrived, but also because, once again, he might fail to discover the identity of the secret admirer.

About to make his favorite noodles and binge-watch his preferred series, he heard the doorbell. To his surprise, one of his students, Manasvi, stood there with a worried expression, holding a handful of medicines.

Sushant insisted on having coffee before she left. While in his small yet cozy studio apartment, Manasvi took in the organized space. Only she knew the courage it took to make this decision. Worried about Sushant's health after learning about his sick day, she decided to check on him.

For the first time in her 20 years, Manasvi made a decision for herself. With no one to call her own except her controlling grandmother, she dared to live for herself. Her grandmother forced her into art school, a path she never wanted. Sushant observed her staring blankly at his art pieces on the wall, reminiscent of the first time he saw her.

***

His first memory of her was in the canteen, quietly sitting in a corner. Despite rarely attending classes, she was always in the same spot each morning.

Sushant, known for scolding students for bunking classes, found himself unable to reprimand her due to the perpetual sadness in her eyes. Over time, he discovered her story, eventually sparking her interest in drawings.

While handing her a coffee cup, Sushant accidentally knocked off her bag, scattering its contents on the floor. As he picked up the items, he noticed calligraphic handwritten postcards similar to the ones he received. To his surprise, Sushant realized that his secret admirer was Manasvi, the most shy and introverted girl.

Returning the contents to her bag, he handed the coffee cup to Manasvi, bringing her out of her thoughts. He smiled, recognizing her as a sweet and interesting girl who seldom confided in others. Their bond deepened over months, starting when he supported her during an argument with her grandmother. The turning point was when he found her sitting alone at the beach, lost and in tears. Holding her tight, he comforted her, marking the beginning of their bond.

Manasvi realized she admired Sushant, keeping it a secret until now. She hoped that one day she would openly admit her feelings to Sushant. ♡

About the Authors

Juju's Pearls (Dr. Reemanshu Bansal)

Dr. Reemanshu Bansal, a prominent figure from New Delhi, India, is a distinguished Radiologist, Author, Blogger, Book Coach, and Social activist. An alumnus of Tata Memorial Hospital, Mumbai, she balances her roles as a Radiologist and Author, with 21 books, including the Momsie Popsie Diary series. Founder of JRC-Juju's Reader Club and JRC Mobile Library, she actively supports social causes, earning 25 awards and recognition on Amazon. Beyond literature, Dr. Bansal attracts attention from OTT platforms and film events. Learn more at *reemanshu.blogspot.com* or contact her at *reemanshu2003@gmail.com*.

Manmohan Sadana

Manmohan Sadana, a retired Joint Director General (Tourism) from the Government of India, is a versatile individual with accomplishments as an author, editor, actor, and mandolinist. His novel, "Healing Strings," has garnered acclaim, receiving prestigious awards such as the "Literary Titan Gold Award," "Golden Book Award," "Ukiyoto Emerging Author Award," "Certificate of Appreciation from Kerala Tourism Mart Society," and the esteemed "Ukiyoto Book of the Decade Award."

Yogesh A Gupta

Dr. Yogesh Gupta, a senior doctor based in Ahmedabad, India, emphasizes through this short story that the essence of love cannot be truly understood without delving into the narrative he shares.

Sabbani Laxminarayana

Sabbani Laxminarayana, a retired Junior Lecturer from Telangana, has a prolific literary career with 36 Telugu books covering poetry, fiction, and nonfiction. Proficient in Telugu, Hindi, and English, he received numerous awards, including Best Teacher Award and Nava Srujan Kala Praveen Award. Acknowledged by Telangana Book of Records, he won the "Azadi ka Amrit Mahotsav" Desh Bhakti Geet State level Second Prize in 2022. Contact him at In.sabbani@gmail.com or +918985251271.

Riddhima Sen

Riddhima Sen is presently pursuing Comparative Literature at Jadavpur University. She is a versatile individual, excelling as an author, artist, and host.

Shaurya Prakash

Shaurya Prakash, a Grade XI student at Scindia School, harbors a profound and intellectual passion for literature and poetry. He takes delight in the art of crafting poetry, using a distinctive and eloquent voice to express his thoughts and emotions. As a published author, his short story is featured in the book "Blazing Dreams." With aspirations of becoming a lawyer, Shaurya seamlessly combines his keen literary mind with a dedicated commitment to comprehending and articulating the intricacies of human life.

Purnima Dixit

Purnima is a heartfelt writer, weaving thoughts into words and expressing emotions through her captivating prose. Her passion for simplicity is evident as she articulates her experiences and opinions on subjects that captivate her interest. Holding a post-graduate degree in literature, Purnima's love for reading has fueled her journey into writing. Starting with simple reviews of TV episodes on WordPress, she transitioned to crafting fictional stories and eventually found her voice in poetry. With a writing journey that began in 2015, Purnima aspires to pursue her passion as a dedicated writer. When she's not immersed in the world of words, you can find her indulging in good music, reading, and, most importantly, enjoying Korean dramas.

www.ingramcontent.com/pod-product-compliance
Lightning Source LLC
LaVergne TN
LVHW041549070526
838199LV00046B/1884